MADNESS
IN THE MINE

MADNESS
IN THE MINE
AN UNOFFICIAL MINECRAFTERS
TIME TRAVEL ADVENTURE
BOOK FIVE

Winter Morgan

Sky Pony Press
New York

Copyright © 2019 by Hollan Publishing, Inc.

Minecraft® is a registered trademark of Notch Development AB.

The Minecraft game is copyright © Mojang AB.

All rights reserved. No part of this book may be reproduced in any manner without the express written consent of the publisher, except in the case of brief excerpts in critical reviews or articles. All inquiries should be addressed to Sky Pony Press, 307 West 36th Street, 11th Floor, New York, NY 10018.

Sky Pony Press books may be purchased in bulk at special discounts for sales promotion, corporate gifts, fund-raising, or educational purposes. Special editions can also be created to specifications. For details, contact the Special Sales Department, Sky Pony Press, 307 West 36th Street, 11th Floor, New York, NY 10018 or info@skyhorsepublishing.com.

Sky Pony® is a registered trademark of Skyhorse Publishing, Inc.®, a Delaware corporation.

Minecraft® is a registered trademark of Notch Development AB.
The Minecraft game is copyright © Mojang AB.

Visit our website at www.skyponypress.com.

10 9 8 7 6 5 4 3 2 1

Library of Congress Cataloging-in- Publication Data is available on file.

Cover design by Brian Peterson
Cover art by Megan Miller

Print ISBN: 978-1-5107-4118-8
E-book ISBN: 978-1-5107-4131-7

Printed in Canada

TABLE OF CONTENTS

MADNESS IN THE MINE

OLD HABITS

Brett couldn't believe he landed his dream project. He had often walked past the patch of land next to his friend Helen's house and wished he could transform the grassy area into a massive farm. He had even imagined how it would look and what could be grown there. He was elated when Helen reached out and told him that she wanted to create a farm on the patch of land next to her house.

"Really, Helen?" asked Brett.

"Yes." Helen pushed her long red hair from her face. "I know the town has a farm, but I think I should have my own. Especially since I have this large space next to my house. Although I love the town farm, when I'm there, I have to pay attention to how many apples and potatoes I take so there is enough food for everyone. If I have my own farm, I can pick apples whenever I want them."

Brett agreed. "Helen, this is a smart idea."

"Obviously you can help yourself to the crops once the farm is finished. I don't mind sharing," Helen said.

"Thanks." Brett rattled off a list of ideas for the farm, mentioning an irrigation system, seeds, and carrots as Helen nodded her head.

"It seems like you have a lot of ideas," she remarked. "Maybe you'd like to invite Joe to Meadow Mews. He can help you build the farm."

"That sounds like a wonderful idea." Brett was eager to tell Joe. It had been a while since he worked with Joe, and he missed having his friend beside him while he strategized how to develop the farm and planted seeds.

"Great. When can you get started?" asked Helen.

Before Brett could reply, Poppy sprinted over to them. "Brett! Helen!" she called out. "I have some incredible news!"

"What is it?" Helen asked.

"The town has asked me to build a skyscraper," she blurted out. Her voice was excited and high-pitched.

"Wow!" Brett and Helen said in unison.

Helen added, "This would be a great addition to Meadow Mews. How tall will it be? And will you create a place atop the skyscraper where we could take in the view of the town and the sea below?"

"I hadn't thought of that, but that sounds like a great idea!" said Poppy.

Brett suggested, "A lot of new buildings have rooftop farms. Perhaps I can build one in this skyscraper and we can use it to feed the workers in the building."

"You guys have the best ideas," exclaimed Poppy.

Helen said, "Speaking of farms, Brett is creating a farm next to my house."

"Wonderful." Poppy looked at the land next to Helen's house. "I've always thought it was the perfect place to build a farm."

"I'm going to ask Joe to help me build it. Would you be interested in traveling to Farmer's Bay to see him?" asked Brett.

"I'd love to," Poppy replied. "I don't have to start building the skyscraper until next week, and I have a bunch of free time, which is rare for me."

Brett chuckled. Poppy wasn't the type of person who had free time. She was always in the middle of a project. He was happy that she was able to join him on this trip. They had both been so busy with work, they couldn't see each other as much as they used to. In fact, it had been months since they had pulled one of their famous pranks. Brett hoped they could come up with great ideas for pranks while they walked toward Farmer's Bay.

"Helen," asked Brett, "when do you want me to begin work on the farm?"

"As soon as you can," she replied.

Poppy suggested they leave straight away for Farmer's Bay, and Brett agreed. They stopped at the community farm on the way and picked some fruit for their inventory. Brett and Poppy were mindful that they didn't take too much fruit.

"Helen told me that I could use her farm," said Brett.

"I hope she lets me use it too," said Poppy.

They ate apples they had just picked as they walked along the grassy landscape and made their way along the coast. They could see a large boat off in the distance.

"Look at that boat." Poppy pointed out the large wooden ship. "It looks like a pirate ship. I wonder where it will dock."

"It looks like it's heading toward Farmer's Bay," said Brett as he took a final bite from his apple.

"Let's not talk about the boat," said Poppy with a sinister look on her face. "We have to think about planning a new prank. I feel like we haven't pulled one off for ages. Remember the pranking contest? We should do something like that again."

Brett remembered the pranking contest and how it didn't work out the way they planned. "Yes," he said. "We need to do something a little less staged. Let's pull a prank on Joe."

"Good idea!" Poppy smirked. "Maybe we can pretend we're ghosts and make noise, but hide. He will hear noises, but nobody will be there."

"That's a plan," Brett laughed.

"Let's take a potion of Invisibility," Poppy said.

"Yes, that's perfect."

The sun was beginning to set when they reached Farmer's Bay. They sprinted toward Joe's bungalow near the dock. Poppy had recently built the bungalow for Joe. He loved it because she had placed a large picture window that looked out to the bay, and he loved waking up every morning and seeing what was going on at the pier.

Joe was brewing potions when they arrived at his bungalow. They swallowed the potion of Invisibility and then knocked on the window. When Joe looked out to see who was there, they bolted away. Then they knocked on his door. Joe walked outside his door to see if anybody was there, but there was nobody at his door. Joe shrugged and went back to crafting potions. Then he heard yet another knock on his window. He sighed as he looked out at the setting sun. He didn't see anybody at the window, but he did notice a large ship docking in Farmer's Bay.

"Wow," he said to himself, "that's some ship. I hope it's not filled with pirates."

He stared at the boat, and he heard another knock at his door. He hoped it wasn't someone from the ship. The ship had a skull and crossbones flag, and this upset Joe. He didn't think anybody traveling on the ship would be nice. It looked like the type of vessel that transported people who liked to loot and take over the town.

Joe opened the door, but again there was nobody there. He called out, "Hi, Brett! Hi, Poppy! What a surprise. I wasn't expecting you to visit."

"What?" Poppy replied, but she was confused.

"How did you know it was us?" Brett called out.

"Just a good guess," Joe said as Brett and Poppy's potion wore off and they appeared at his front door. "You better get in here soon because it's getting dark, and you wouldn't want to be attacked by a hostile mob. We had a skeleton attack last night that was intense. I am hoping that doesn't happen again tonight."

"A skeleton attack?" questioned Poppy.

"Yes, there were tons of skeletons in the town and everybody had to go out and fight them. It was exhausting."

"We had something like that a few weeks ago," said Brett.

Poppy added, "It only lasted one night."

"Well, hopefully this skeleton attack was only one night too," Brett said, then offered them some food. "I have a bunch of cake. Would you like a slice?"

"Yes," they both replied.

"I assume you are going to stay here tonight. It's too late to travel back to Meadow Mews," Joe said as he cut them a slice of cake.

"Yes," Brett said. "I actually came here because I wanted to ask you to help me build a farm next to Helen's house."

"She finally wants to build the farm you've always dreamed about?" Joe asked.

"Yes." Brett smiled.

"That's great news. I'd love to build it with you."

Poppy added, "When you're done with the farm, I was hoping you could help me build a rooftop farm on top of a skyscraper I am building in Meadow Mews."

"Yes." Joe's eyes widened. "That sounds like a fascinating project. This is so exciting. I'm thrilled you guys came by."

As they ate cake, someone opened the door to Joe's bungalow. They quickly put on their armor and grabbed their diamond swords. They were ready to battle skeletons, but as they raced toward the door, they weren't met by any bony beasts. Instead a group of five people wearing masks stood at Joe's door.

Joe aimed his diamond sword at them and asked, "What do you want?"

They didn't reply.

2

SHIPS

The masked people leaped with diamond swords at the gang while also splashing potions on them. "Who are you?" hollered Poppy as she jumped back to avoid being splashed by the potion. The gang didn't respond. They just struck the group.

Joe struck one of the masked people with his diamond sword, destroying him. This infuriated the gang, who fought even harder. They splashed a potion of Harming on Poppy, Joe, and Brett, leaving each of them with one heart.

"What do you want from us?" Brett questioned. He was weak, and his voice was low.

"Everything from your house," demanded one of the attackers.

Brett noticed the attacker had an explorer map in his hand. He had only heard about these new maps and how they helped adventurers find buried treasure. "Are you looking for buried treasure? If so, you should focus on mining on the beach and not bothering us. Whatever we have won't be as valuable as buried treasure."

"That's none of your business," the person replied and placed the explorer map in his inventory.

"I don't have much," said Joe. "I was in the middle of brewing potions because I don't have any in my inventory. I also traded all of my emeralds and other valuables to get the supplies for my friend Poppy to build this bungalow. She just built it a few weeks ago."

"We don't care to hear about your house. We want whatever you have. First give us all of your diamond swords and whatever weapons you have," they demanded.

"Why are you wearing masks?" asked Poppy. "Are you too scared to show your real faces?"

"I should destroy you for that comment, but then I couldn't get all of your loot. Now, stop asking questions and give me everything you have." They held a sword to Poppy's head.

"I'd rather you destroy me than take my stuff. You guys are a bunch of bullies." Poppy wouldn't budge and didn't remove anything from her inventory.

"I might have used command blocks to put you on hardcore mode. Aren't you nervous?" The criminal chuckled as they pressed the sword into Poppy's brown braids.

"I will take my chances." She smiled.

Brett was in awe of Poppy's fearlessness. He wished he could be that brave. He wondered if the attackers actually did put the town on hardcore mode, meaning they could be destroyed forever. He began to shake. "Poppy," Brett said, "just hand over all of your stuff."

Poppy was about to hand over her sword when one of the invaders cried out in pain. "My shoulder!"

"Oh no!" one of the criminals yelled. "Skeletons!"

Joe was never so relieved to see the town invaded by skeletons. He used the opportunity to grab a bottle of milk from his inventory and gulp some down. Then he handed it to his friends.

Poppy and Brett drank the milk and regained their energy. They had to battle both the skeletons and the criminals. Using their swords, they slammed into a masked invader who stood in Joe's doorway until he was destroyed.

"Now it's a fair battle," said Brett. "There are three of them and three of us."

"There's nothing fair about this. These people are attacking us and trying to steal all of our possessions," said Poppy.

"We also have to find out if they put us on hard-core mode." Joe took a deep breath as he spoke and then leaped at one of the criminals battling a skeleton.

A skeleton's arrow struck Joe's shoulder and he wailed. He took another sip of milk and lunged at the skeleton, obliterating the bony beast. As he reached toward the ground to pick up a bone, he spotted Brett destroying two criminals and Poppy striking the final one. He felt relieved until he looked up. "What is that?" he shouted.

A winged beast flew above them. It wasn't the Ender Dragon or a Wither, and he wasn't certain what this beast was and how they should destroy it. The bluish gray beast swooped down toward Joe, and he swung his diamond sword at its side, but the blow only weakened the winged beast and didn't destroy it. The beast eyed Joe again as it swooped toward him for a second time. Joe pierced the wing, injuring the flying mob and then destroying it. A weird substance dropped to the ground.

"That's phantom membranes," Ray, an alchemist from Farmer's Bay, called out to Joe. "Pick it up. It's rare and very valuable."

Ray destroyed a skeleton and raced toward Joe. "You can make a potion of Slow Falling with phantom membranes. If you take that potion, you will be able to fall and not get hurt. It's such an incredible potion. I sell out of it very quickly. In fact, I'd trade you a ton of potions for the phantom membranes," said Ray.

Joe wasn't in the mood to trade. It was the middle of the night, and his friends, as well as the rest of the residents of Farmer's Bay, were dealing with a second night of skeleton invasions. He was tired and yawned.

"You haven't been sleeping, right?" asked Ray.

Joe couldn't believe Ray was having such a casual conversation in the midst of an epic battle. Didn't he understand skeletons surrounded them and more were spawning by the minute? A skeleton arrow hit Joe's arm, and Ray turned around and struck the skeleton with his diamond sword. As Ray destroyed the skeleton, the sun came up, and all of the skeletons disappeared.

"What was that beast that attacked you?" asked Poppy.

"Who were those masked people who tried to rob us?" asked Brett.

These questions swam around Joe's head, and he felt like he was about to collapse.

"Joe isn't sleeping," explained Ray. "That creature is called the Phantom, and it attacks people who haven't slept in over three days. I have to make myself stay up to spawn it so I can use the phantom membranes it drops when it's destroyed. Speaking of which, can I have some of that potion?"

"Are you not sleeping?" asked Poppy.

"No, I haven't. Last night I was up battling skeletons, and the other two nights I was working on my potions and didn't realize I had to sleep until the sun came up. I really lost track of time," replied Joe.

"Well that's not good," said Brett, "You're going to have to get some sleep."

"Don't go to sleep right away," suggested Ray. "If you stay up you'll be able to spawn another Phantom, and we can get more membranes."

"I don't want to spawn Phantoms," said Joe. "I have to leave with Brett and Poppy and work on two farms."

"Yes," said Poppy. "Joe is coming to Meadow Mews with us."

"Meadow Mews," said Ray. "I've heard that town needs an alchemist."

"That's true," said Brett. "Ours has been traveling, searching for ingredients. His friend was supposed to sell potions when he was away, but he hasn't been selling them."

"I'd like to come with you guys and sell potions in Meadow Mews. Business has been slow here. It seems like people in Farmer's Bay like to brew their own potions, even if it means that they lose sleep," he said as he stared at Joe.

"I like brewing potions," confessed Joe. "I'm sorry I'm not buying them from you."

Poppy said, "We should get back to town. You guys have to start working on Helen's farm."

"Let me just get my case, and I'll join you," said Ray.

As the gang waited for Ray, Poppy spotted something on the floor. She picked it up. "Oh my, look those criminals dropped their explorer map."

Her two friends crowded around her and studied the map. Joe said, "It looks like there's buried treasure on the beach. It's right next to us."

"We should dig and find it," said Poppy.

"Yes," said Brett. "After everything they did to us, we deserve to get their treasure."

Ray raced toward them. "Why are you guys heading toward the beach? I thought you were going to Meadow Mews."

"We have to dig up a treasure before we go," Poppy pointed to the map.

Once they reached the beach, the gang pulled out their pickaxes and began to dig. The sun beat down on them, and sweat formed on their brows. They dug into the sandy beach, but there wasn't any treasure.

"Are you sure this map is correct?" asked Ray. "Where did you find it?"

Before any of them could respond, they saw the treasure chest. Joe pulled it out from the ground and opened it. The chest was teeming with gold ingots. As they picked up a gold ingot, a voice called out, "That's ours."

3
TREASURE

"Who are they?" asked Ray.

"We don't know," Joe said as he looked at the five masked people. "Maybe if you guys take off your masks, we might be able to recognize you."

"I guess they didn't put everyone on hardcore mode last night, or they wouldn't have respawned," said Poppy.

"Hardcore mode?" Ray shivered as he spoke.

One of the criminals took off the blue cloth mask that covered her nose and mouth and pulled out her hat. She had orange hair and green eyes. She said, "Now will you give us our treasure?"

Joe handed a gold ingot to the woman. "I am not taking something that isn't mine. I don't steal like you guys do."

Ray was confused and asked, "What's going on?"

Joe explained how these masked criminals appeared at his door the previous night and demanded all of their stuff from their inventories.

"That's horrible," said Ray. "They don't deserve this treasure. They should be put in the bedrock prison in Farmer's Bay."

"We didn't take anything," said the orange-headed woman. "Unlike you guys, who took our treasure map and are now holding our gold ingots. We apologize for surprising you last night. We won't attack you. Just leave us with our treasure."

Ray said, "It doesn't work that way." He looked at the ship docked at Farmer's Bay and asked, "Is that your boat?"

"Yes," she replied.

"Take your treasure and never come back to our town. I am going to warn other people around the Overworld about you guys. You are pirates, and nobody wants pirates showing up and looting their town."

"Fine," the woman said as she picked up the large treasure chest and walked back to the ship with her four masked friends following closely behind.

Ray and the others watched them board the ship and it sailed away. "Those guys are awful," said Joe.

"I can't believe we let them leave with the treasure." Poppy was annoyed.

"It was their map," Joe reminded them. "I'm just glad they're gone."

Brett said, "I assume they didn't put this town on hardcore mode."

Ray shrieked, "Did they say they put the town on hardcore mode? That's crazy. We shouldn't have let them leave."

"I think it was just a threat," said Poppy. "I don't believe it."

"Well, it's too late to find out now," said Ray. His voice shook as he spoke. He was worried they would be destroyed.

"We could look for the command blocks," said Poppy.

"I think we should head to Meadow Mews and work on the farm," said Joe. "They could be anywhere, and we might never find them. Also, I don't believe those guys would do anything that extreme."

"For example, they didn't have to ask for the treasure back. They could have just destroyed us, and then we'd be gone from the Overworld. That would be much easier," said Brett.

"Let's not debate this all day," said Poppy. "We should go home."

Ray lugged his large case of potions as they left Farmer's Bay and made their way to Meadow Mews. As they approached the town, Brett pointed out the large ship docked in the distance. "It looks as if they docked their boat at Meadow Mews."

The gang sprinted toward the dock and climbed aboard the ship, but it was empty. As they searched the cavernous wooden ship, they spotted a room filled with treasure chests.

"Wow, these guys are serious treasure hunters," said Ray.

"Look at how many maps they have," said Poppy as she pointed to a stack of explorer maps. "They must spend a lot of time under the sea."

"I wonder what they are doing in Meadow Mews. We should get off the boat and stop them from damaging the town," said Brett.

The gang hurried down the stairs and into the middle of the village. They passed the library, and Heather the librarian came out and spoke to them.

"I just had the strangest interaction today," said Heather.

"What happened?" asked Poppy.

"Some woman with orange hair came into the library and asked for all of the books on the history of Meadow Mews. She said she was going to destroy them because she plans on destroying it and rewriting the town's history."

"We know her," said Poppy. "She's awful. We will stop her."

"I wouldn't let her take a book out. She can't destroy our town," she said.

"She won't," Brett reassured Heather.

Ray was more concerned with starting his business. As Poppy, Brett, and Joe looked around the town for the criminals, he asked if he should set up his business in the middle of the village.

"You can do what you like." Joe was annoyed. "We have a situation on our hands, and I assume you don't want to solve it."

"I'm sorry," said Ray. "I didn't know you needed my help."

"We need everyone's help," said Joe.

As the four of them walked through the village, searching for the folks that want to destroy Meadow Mews and rewrite the history, Helen called out to them.

"You guys are back. Are you going to start on the farm today?"

"We'd like to, but we have to find some people who want to invade Meadow Mews," explained Brett.

"Who would want to destroy Meadow Mews?" asked Helen. She was shocked.

"The people who are traveling on that ship," said Poppy. She pointed toward the water, but the ship was missing.

"What ship?" asked Helen. "Are you sure you guys are okay?

"There was a large wooden ship docked at the waterfront. Didn't you see it?" asked Poppy.

"No, I didn't," replied Helen.

Poppy, Brett, Joe, and Ray were confused. Brett said, "The ship was there, and Heather the librarian described a woman we know who is traveling on that ship."

"I don't know what you are talking about. Perhaps you guys should go home and rest and then start on the farm tomorrow. You guys don't look too well," said Helen.

"No, we're fine," said Joe. "We can start today."

Since the ship was gone, the gang assumed the criminals had gotten what they needed and left. Ray set up his potion stand in the center of town, Poppy went home to draft up designs for the skyscraper, and Brett and Joe walked outside of the village toward Helen's house. As they passed a large mine, they spotted a woman with orange hair entering the mine.

"Did you see that?" asked Brett.

"See what?" asked Helen.

"I saw a woman entering that mine," replied Brett.

"That mine?" Helen questioned with a chuckle. "Nobody has used that mine for ages. You know that it has nothing in it. Hasn't ever since I've been in the town, and I've been here for ages. As you both know."

Brett remembered how he had fallen into a portal, seen Helen in the past, and fought a battle with her to keep the town standing. He had forgotten that the mine had been emptied all the way back then. He wondered what the orange-haired woman wanted in the mine. He had to go inside and find out. He readjusted his armor and said, "I'm sorry, but I have to check out this mine before we head to your house to build the farm."

Helen smiled. "That's fine. I haven't been in this mine for a long time. I used to come here because I was convinced that eventually it would be replenished with minerals and I'd be the first to mine all the diamonds and emeralds, but that never happened. I would just go inside and wind up battling a cave spider, and then I'd leave empty-handed."

"Do you know why the mine is empty?" asked Joe. "Do you think it's cursed?"

"Cursed?" Brett was shocked. He couldn't believe his friend thought a place could be cursed.

"Yes, why not?" asked Joe.

"I don't believe in curses," replied Brett.

"Why not?" Joe questioned.

"Because they aren't real," said Brett.

"Guys." Helen wanted to defuse this potential debate on the legitimacy of curses. She said, "There are many stories about the mine and what happened to it. Some of them do involve curses. We have no answers for why this mine has been emptied and nothing grows there. We can make up any story we want, but we will never know the truth. Whenever this mine became emptied, it was way before any inhabitant settled in Meadow Mews. Before Grant settled the town and Connor tried to destroy it. This predates everything we know."

Brett said, "Well, I saw that woman go in here, and I want to see what she is up to."

Brett pulled a torch from his inventory and walked into the mine. He spotted a cave spider and slammed it with his sword.

"I told you," Helen said. "The only things in this cave are spiders. There's nothing else."

Joe looked at the hole in the ground. There were no signs of diamonds or other mining finds. It was barren.

"She's right," said Joe.

They heard a sound of someone digging into the ground with a pickaxe in the distance. Brett rushed toward the sound until he heard someone scream, "Stop! Don't move!"

4

MINED

Brett didn't listen and kept tearing through the mine. The voice called out again, "I'm warning you. Please don't move. You will get hurt." Brett kept running.

Joe spotted command blocks. He walked toward them and slammed his diamond sword into them. "These command blocks are probably being used to put us on hardcore mode." He screamed as he destroyed the blocks.

"Stop!" A masked criminal lunged toward Joe and struck him with a diamond sword while also splashing a potion of Harming on him. Joe had one heart left. He stopped destroying the cubes because he worried that they had put players on hardcore mode, and he feared being destroyed forever.

"What are you doing with these blocks?" asked Joe.

"That's none of your business," said the masked criminal.

"Where did your ship go?" asked Joe.

"Again, that is also none of your business. Stop asking questions," the masked criminal pointed his sword at Joe. "With one more strike, you will be gone." He laughed.

Joe tried to pull a bottle of milk from his inventory, but his hands were shaky. He finally was able to get a bottle and took a sip. "I don't understand what you want from us."

"I want nothing from you but to leave us alone. Get out of here," said the criminal.

Helen hid in the corner. Nobody had seen her, but now two cave spiders were crawling near her leg, and she had to attack them. She swung her sword at the cave spiders, and the masked criminal called out, "Who is over there?"

"Leave her alone," Joe pleaded. "She's our friend. She didn't even want to go into this mine."

"She's intruding," said the criminal.

"You don't own this mine," Joe reminded him.

"Didn't I tell you to stop talking?" the criminal asked Joe and then sprinted toward Helen.

"Please don't hit me," Helen said. "I'll leave. I just want to find my friend Brett."

Brett called out, "Helen, get out. This is a trap."

Joe sprinted toward Brett's voice. He had to help his friend get out of whatever trap he was in. Helen battled the masked criminal by the cave's entrance. As they battled, a loud, thunderous boom shook the town and rain fell hard in the ground outside the cave. A crop of skeletons spawned by the cave's entrance and began attacking Helen and the criminal. The criminal was weak, then had only one heart left, then was destroyed.

Helen sprinted back into the cave. She could see Joe and Brett battling the woman with orange hair, and she rushed in their direction, but she dropped her torch and couldn't see. She ran in the darkness, but she tripped and fell down a large hole. Helen screamed for help, but she felt as if she didn't make a sound. Helen had never felt this cold in her life. Her body shivered, and her skin felt like it was covered in ice. She tried to imagine herself on a warm beach, but nothing helped. She was cold, and she was quite sure she might freeze to death.

When she landed after falling in the seemingly never-ending hole, she landed with a large thump. She looked around. It appeared that she was still in the mine, but this mine was filled with diamonds. She pulled out her pickaxe and began to dig into the blocks.

Although Helen wasn't certain where she landed, she knew that she had to make the best of the situation. She had never been in a mine that had so many diamonds. It seemed like every time she banged her pickaxe into the ground, she uncovered another cluster of diamonds. A voice called out, "Is there anyone in here?"

The voice sounded familiar, but she couldn't quite place it. She didn't reply. She grabbed milk to replenish her energy, traded in her pickaxe for a diamond sword, and walked toward the sound of the voice.

"Hello," the voice said.

Helen smiled when she saw Grant standing by the entrance. It had been a long time since she saw her old friend. "Grant!"

Grant looked confused. "Do I know you?"

"Yes." She smiled. "It's your friend Helen. I haven't seen you in ages."

"I don't think we've ever met," he said. "I'm sorry if we did and I don't remember you."

Helen thought about the portal. She recalled the first time she met Brett and Joe and how they had said they were from the future. She trusted they were telling the truth but didn't know if they were until she met them in their time period. Now she was meeting an old friend in a similar way. She wasn't sure how she could explain this to him. Instead of telling him she was from the future, she just said, "It's okay if you have forgotten me. We met only briefly."

"Isn't this mine great?" asked Grant. "I feel like I can mine here every day and it never gets emptied. It's like a gift to the Overworld. I am using all of the resources I gather from this mine to start a town. I want to call it Meadow Mews."

"That's a good name. I'm sure it will stick," Helen said with a chuckle.

"Why are you laughing?" Grant questioned.

"Oh, no reason. Sorry." Helen walked out of the mine and into the sunlight. It was nice to be in the sun. She still had a chill from when she fell down into the portal.

"Would you like something to eat?" asked Grant. "I just made a big lunch."

Helen followed her old friend toward his home, then she heard someone call out to her.

"Helen!"

She turned around and saw Joe and Brett jogging toward her. "Where are we?" asked Brett.

"What time period is this?" asked Joe.

Grant walked toward them, and Joe and Brett both said in unison, "We are in the past."

Brett looked at the landscape. There was one solitary house in the distance, which he recognized as Grant's house. He said, "We are in the way past. Like, well before we were here the last time."

"What are you talking about?" asked Grant.

Helen ignored Grant and told Brett and Joe, "We are here before the mine was emptied."

"The mine will be empty?" questioned Grant.

"Yes," said Joe.

"How do you know? Who are you?" asked Grant.

Joe said, "I'm Joe, and this is my friend Brett. I come from a town called Farmer's Bay."

Grant interrupted him, "Farmer's Bay?"

"Yes," said Joe.

"I have plans to create a town called Farmer's Bay. I made a map and everything," exclaimed Grant.

"It's farther down the coastline." Joe looked around the grassy meadow and wasn't sure which direction

Farmer's Bay would be in. There were no buildings to help him find his way. He usually used landmarks, like Poppy's gorgeous castle, to guide him.

Grant pointed toward the left. "Down that way. Yes, I have a few people there who are helping me settle the town. But I don't recognize you."

"We are from the future," said Joe.

"Wow," said Grant.

Joe, Brett, and Helen weren't sure if he believed them, but he did invite everyone to his house to have lunch. As they approached Grant's house, he saw his door was open.

"Who is in my house?" asked Grant.

"Maybe you left the door open?" suggested Helen.

"No, I'd never do such a thing," said Grant.

Grant sprinted toward the house and rushed through the door. The woman with orange hair and one of the masked criminals stood by an opened chest. They looked up at Grant and pointed their diamond swords at him.

"Don't get any closer!" the orange-haired woman warned.

5

JOURNEY TO THE PAST

"What are you doing?" Grant hollered. "Get away from my stuff!"

"It's ours now," the woman with orange hair laughed.

The masked criminal pulled out a bow and arrow and aimed at Grant. The arrow ripped into Grant's stomach, and he cried out in pain.

Brett, Joe, and Helen leaped at the two criminals, striking them with diamond swords. When they each had one heart left, the masked criminal cried out, "Stop! Don't destroy us!"

The woman with the orange hair asked weakly, "Before you destroy us, can you tell us where we are? It looks like the town we were in was destroyed, and I don't see our boat. We fell down a hole, and we need to make our way back to the boat."

Brett felt bad for this woman. Even though she was

trying to destroy them and probably spent most of her life traveling around the Overworld robbing people, he knew what it was like to fall through a portal for the first time. The first time he fell down the portal and wound up in the past, he was scared and worried that he'd never get back home. Even now, despite traveling to the past and the future, he was still nervous that he wouldn't make it back home. He rarely enjoyed time travel, and he didn't like that he lacked control over these journeys. He never knew when he'd slip down a portal. He also knew that wherever he landed, there was a reason for it. He was called on this trip to help people. He wondered what role these two criminals had in this time period. Brett didn't say any of this or express these emotions. Instead he asked, "What are your names?"

"I'm Bea," the woman replied.

The other criminal took off her mask. She had bright red eyes and striking silver hair. She said, "I'm Vera."

Bea said, "I'm sorry we have attacked you, but neither of us have any potions or milk in our inventories, and we only have one heart left each. We could be destroyed with another strike from your sword or an attack from a hostile mob. Is it possible you could give us something, even food, to help us replenish our health and hearts?"

Vera added, "We worry if we are destroyed here, we won't respawn."

"Is that because you put Meadow Mews on hardcore mode?" asked Brett.

Grant screamed, "You put Meadow Mews on hard-core mode? And we're supposed to help you?"

"I don't think it worked," confessed Vera.

"I know you guys destroyed most of the command blocks," said Bea.

"What was your plan? What did you want to do to Meadow Mews?" asked Brett.

"We were just following orders," said Vera.

"From whom?" asked Brett.

Vera was about to respond when a loud noise boomed and shook Grant's small house. They sprinted out of the house to find smoke pouring out of the mine.

"What happened?" asked Grant. "Did someone blow up the mine?"

They bolted toward the mine when they saw the Wither flying above the mine's entrance.

"Is that what caused the explosion?" asked Vera.

"What is that?" questioned Bea.

The three-headed beast shot a succession of wither skulls at them. One of the skulls landed by Bea's feet, nearly destroying her.

Brett was surprised at himself when he handed both Bea and Vera bottles of milk and instructed them to drink. "You don't want to get destroyed."

Joe shot an arrow at the Wither and told the Bea and Vera, "That's the Wither, and it's very powerful. We have to destroy it, or it will destroy us."

Brett added, "I can't believe you've never seen a Wither."

"We don't live in this biome," said Bea as she followed closely behind Brett. She shot arrows and mimicked all of his actions while she tried to figure out how to destroy the Wither.

"Where do you live?" asked Joe as he struck the side of the Wither, weakening the beast.

"Under the water. We have a whole different slew of mobs. Have you guys ever had to destroy a Drowned?" Vera asked.

"No," said Joe, "but I've heard about them."

"I haven't, and I didn't even know you could live under the sea," said Grant.

"This is all in the future. You have a lot to look forward to," said Helen as she battled the Wither.

Brett watched Vera and Bea clumsily try to battle the Wither alongside them. He couldn't stop thinking how strange it was to watch these two people, who were attacking them just a few moments ago, battle a mob with them. He wanted to know who sent them into the Overworld to loot and destroy towns. He wondered what their underwater life was like and how they were brought into this criminal world. He also hoped that they would be able to work together to destroy this Wither and to find their way back to their time period.

Joe was the one to deliver the final blow to the Wither, which earned him fifty experience points and a Nether star.

"Good job." Helen smiled.

"Now that the Wither is destroyed, we have to find out who spawned it," said Grant.

"Have you encountered any enemies since you started developing Meadow Mews?" asked Brett.

Helen almost replied for Grant. She almost said, "Connor," but stopped when she remembered all of the issues Grant had with Connor wouldn't happen until much later in the future. She wasn't sure who the enemy was at this point in the past. This time period was never written about. It predated the library. It pre-dated the history books. They were in a time period where they had no clues to help.

Grant thought for a while and responded, "I don't have any enemies that I know of."

The gang made their way toward the mine. As they entered, the smoke dissipated, and they looked at the burned ground.

"This isn't from the Wither," Brett said as he inspected the ground. "It seems like someone must have used TNT."

"Do you see any TNT blocks?" asked Joe as he clutched his torch and walked farther into the mine.

"Not yet," replied Brett.

"I do," Helen called out. She had traveled deep within the mine, so her voice was very faint. "And they haven't been used."

"What?" cried Grant. "Someone can ignite them. Watch out!"

"Okay, but I found something else," said Helen.

They traveled toward the sound of Helen's voice, but they couldn't find her. They held onto their torches until they reached the end of the mine. Helen wasn't there. The only thing they saw was an open door.

6

SURPRISES IN THE
STRONGHOLD

"Helen," Brett called as they walked into a stronghold, but there was no response.

The gang huddled together as they made their way through the dark and musty stronghold.

"You know, I've been to this mine a million times, and I never noticed there was a stronghold," said Grant.

Vera cried out, "Look down!"

The gang let out a collective gasp when they saw the floor of the stronghold was covered with silverfish. The insects bit their feet, and they used their diamond swords to destroy the pesky creatures. As they annihilated the bugs, they heard a noise in the distance.

"Helen?" Brett called out. "We are at the entrance."

Joe added, "Helen, watch where you are walking. There are tons of silverfish."

Helen didn't respond, but the noise grew louder. It sounded as though two people were talking.

"Who's there?" Grant raised his voice.

Again, there was no reply.

Vera and Bea destroyed the final silverfish and lunged deeper into the stronghold to find out where the noise was coming from. As Brett trailed behind them, he wondered if they should trust Vera and Bea. Just because they took off their masks and revealed their true identities didn't mean they were his friends. They could be leading everyone into a trap.

"I see something!" Bea yelled.

"Is it Helen?" asked Brett.

"No," Vera replied.

Brett, Joe, and Grant hurried toward the women, then heard an explosion. Joe turned around to see a creeper explode inches from his body. "I could have been destroyed!"

"And we don't know where you'd respawn," Grant suggested. "After we find Helen, we should all sleep in my house so we know where we will respawn if we're destroyed."

"You mean if we're not on hardcore mode," said Brett.

"We have to remain positive and not assume we are on hardcore mode," said Joe.

The group sprinted down the hall, but they couldn't find Bea and Vera. "Perhaps they disappeared like Helen," said Grant.

"Vera! Bea! Helen!" Joe hollered, but there was no response.

Brett spotted an open door. "I see a room." He raced inside and found himself in a spacious library, with wood-paneled bookshelves covered in cobwebs. He noticed a chest in the corner of the room and opened it.

"Are there gold bars?" asked Joe.

Brett rummaged through the chest. "No, there are papers and books." He inspected the books. "It looks like some of the books are enchanted."

"Wow," said Joe, as Brett handed him a book.

Brett distributed everything from the chest, and when they were finished packing everything into their inventories, they rushed out of the library to find Helen, Bea, and Vera. As they searched the stronghold, they began to grow tired.

"How big is this stronghold?" Brett asked as they walked down another flight of stairs, revealing a floor with a small jail cell.

"Help!" Helen called out.

Helen was trapped on the other side of the cell. Brett pulled at the bars on the cell, but they wouldn't budge.

"Who put you in here?" asked Joe.

"I don't know. I heard an explosion behind me, and as I raced from the smoke, someone pushed me in here. There was so much smoke, I couldn't see them."

"We will get you out," Joe said as he banged his pickaxe against the bars, but nothing seemed to work.

"I can't stay in here a minute longer." Helen's voice cracked. "I have one heart left, and there are so many cave spiders." She slammed her sword into a cave spider that crawled next to her. "If I'm attacked, I will be destroyed."

Grant was finally able to open the door to the jail cell using his diamond sword. He swung his sword into the bars, and they opened.

"Thank you," Helen said.

Before they could sprint out of the stronghold, a group of creepers silently crept down the dirt path and exploded, destroying Helen.

"Helen!" Brett screamed.

Brett, Joe, and Grant shot arrows at the creepers, but they were overwhelmed by the mobs. Three exploded next to Joe, destroying him. Brett and Grant tirelessly battled the remaining creepers, but more spawned when they were done.

"We need help!" cried Grant.

"Grant!" Bea called out.

Bea and Vera sprinted down the hall and shot a barrage of arrows that destroyed the creatures.

Vera said, "We have to get out of here. There's a person who tried to trap us in a jail cell."

"Who?" asked Grant.

"I don't know. We couldn't see them. They were hidden in smoke," explained Bea.

"That must be the same person who trapped Helen," said Brett.

Grant ordered, "Let's go." They sprinted down the narrow hallway and toward the exit. As they reached the exit from the mine, they realized it was nighttime.

Brett pulled a bottle of milk from his inventory and passed it to his friends. "I want to make sure we have enough energy to battle whatever mobs we encounter on the way back to Grant's house."

Bea was taking her final sip of milk when they heard two familiar voices call out to them.

"Help us!" Helen wailed.

Brett was upset to hear Helen's cries, but he was also happy that she wasn't destroyed. He had been devastated thinking his two friends were destroyed and was relieved to see they were alive.

"Help! Quick!" cried Joe.

Brett and the others sprinted toward them and saw two men with green hair holding diamonds swords at their backs.

"You are our prisoners," the green-haired men declared.

7

THE PRISONERS

"What do you want?" asked Grant calmly.

"We don't answer questions. We ask the questions. Stop talking, you are our prisoner," one of the green-haired men replied.

"Lead us to your dwellings," ordered the other man.

Grant knew his friends would be surprised that he said yes, but he knew every inch of the house. He also knew that there was a trapdoor in his living room. He had to get the green-haired men into the living room and then trap them in the crawl space underneath his living room floor. Grant said, "I don't live far from here. I will show you the way."

It was dark, an ideal environment for hostile mobs. As they walked toward Grant's house, the sound of clanging bones was deafening. An army of skeletons marched toward them. Grant heard their attackers whisper to each other, "What are we going to do?"

A barrage of arrows flew toward the gang, and Brett took out his bow and arrow to battle the skeletons. However, before he aimed at a skeleton, he shot an arrow at one of the green-haired men. Helen and Joe joined in, shooting arrows at the men, and one was destroyed after a few arrows pierced his arm. His friend called out for help, but there was nobody there to help him.

"You can't do mean things to people and not expect to have to pay for it," said Helen as she aimed the final arrow, which destroyed the green-haired man.

They were relieved their enemies were gone, but they still had to battle the skeletons. It seemed as if every time they destroyed one set, another crop of skeletons would spawn.

"This battle is pointless," said Joe. He was exhausted. He hadn't slept in days, and he wondered if a Phantom would spawn because of his insomnia. He was happy when he realized that they were in a time period when Phantoms didn't exist. However, he sighed because skeletons existed in this world, and he would have to battle them until the sun came and lose another night of sleep.

The skeletons surrounded them, and the gang used all the arrows they had to destroy them. Any break they had, they passed around bottles of milk to replenish their energy. They were almost out of milk and energy when the sun came up.

"Is it okay to sleep all day?" Joe yawned as the sun shined on Meadow Mews.

"No," said Brett. "We have to figure out who those people were and why they wanted to trap us."

"They must have something to do with the mine," said Helen.

Bea surprised them when she said, "Those two men looked very familiar."

"What?" questioned Grant.

"I've seen them before. I just can't remember where," Bea said.

"Me too," added Vera. "I have seen them. Do they live under the sea?"

"Yes," replied Bea, "they do!"

"Aren't they friends with—" Vera stopped speaking.

"Friends with whom?" Brett demanded.

Bea warned her friend, "Don't tell him."

"You better tell us," said Helen. "We are all in this together. Those people were going to make you a prisoner."

"If we tell you who our leader is, we will be destroyed. He wants to remain anonymous," explained Vera.

"You are working for a criminal, and he is probably friends with these two men who are destroying a vital resource in the Overworld. We've always wondered what happened to this mine and why it was destroyed," said Helen.

Grant said, "I don't want to live in a world where this is destroyed."

"We have the opportunity to change history," said Helen. "That's rare."

Bea said, "We work for a person who is terrorizing the underwater community. He has been around forever. I think if we go under the sea now, we might be able to stop him before he becomes too powerful."

"That sounds like a great idea," said Brett.

Grant confessed, "I don't know how to swim."

"Have you never been under the sea?" asked Helen.

"No. I've been fishing a few times, but I've heard stories about elder guardians, and I never wanted to go underneath the water. I like being on blocky ground."

Joe understood. He wasn't a fan of underwater life. He knew things progressed in his time period, and there were lots of great ocean monuments that were teeming with treasure, but he also liked to remain on ground. He said, "You guys can dive into the sea, and I can stay here with Grant. We can watch Meadow Mews."

Brett chuckled. "There's nothing here. Meadow Mews doesn't exist yet. But if there is an undersea world that is developing, and if that world could have people who might be responsible for destroying this mine as well as for attacking us in our time period, we have to figure out who is behind it and stop them before they take over."

"What else is going to happen in the future?" Grant's voice cracked as he asked this question. He was nervous.

Brett didn't want to tell him that by the next time they would see him, the mine would already be destroyed. He didn't want to tell Grant about the battle with Connor and how Grant wasn't living in Meadow

Mews anymore. He just said, "There have been a lot of advancements, but there are also issues. There is a chance that we will see you again in the near future."

Joe said, "Are you telling Grant about the other time we went back in time?"

"You guys have time traveled before?" Bea was surprised.

"Yes," said Brett. "To the past and the future."

"That doesn't matter," explained Joe, "because there is also a chance that we will be stuck in this time period forever."

"Do you think we'll be stuck?" Vera was anxious.

"I don't know, but I do know that we could wind up changing history, and if that happens we might never make that first trip back in time," explained Joe.

Brett looked at everyone. "It will be okay. I mean, we are all together, and we all have the same goal. We want to take care of one another and stop the person who is trying to cause harm to others. As long as we have that in common, we will be okay."

Everyone agreed. As they reached Grant's house, they saw the door was open, and the green-haired men were standing in the doorway.

"Our prisoners have returned."

8

TIME TRAVELERS

"We know who you are," said Bea.

"And you're our prisoners," declared Vera as she swung her diamond sword, striking one of the green-haired men.

"You don't know who we are," hollered the other green-haired man as he leaped toward Vera.

"Leave my friend alone." Bea lunged at the man, plunging her sword into his shoulder and destroying him.

The remaining man pleaded, "Stop! Don't attack me!"

Vera put down her sword and pulled a bottle of potion from her inventory. She splashed the potion on him, weakening him and leaving him with one heart. He was frozen and could barely speak. Vera used this opportunity to question the man.

"Why are you here?" she asked calmly.

"I am here to find you," he told Vera.

"Me?" She questioned.

"And Bea," he added.

"How do you know our names?" asked Vera.

"I'm from the future, like you guys." He introduced himself, "I'm Ivan. I also work for Mikayla."

"Who is Mikayla?" questioned Brett.

Bea's voice shook as she said, "That's the person who is in charge of us."

"Mikayla is in charge of the entire undersea community," explained Ivan.

"She is the queen," said Vera, "and she wants to be the queen of the Overworld."

"Wow, there are kings and queens in the future." Grant was stunned.

"No, there aren't," Brett said. "This person, Mikayla, must have declared herself a queen."

"We don't need a queen in the Overworld," said Joe.

"I agree," added Brett.

Bea wasn't focusing on everyone's opinions about Mikayla. Instead she wanted to know how Ivan and his friend were able to travel back in time. Perhaps they knew about a portal where she could travel to the future. She didn't like being in the Overworld, and she couldn't go under the sea and live the life she was used to. The sea world was too primitive.

"How did you get here?" she asked.

"We were trailing behind you guys, and when we saw you fall into the mine, we just jumped in after you," said Ivan.

"So you have no idea how to get back to our time period?" asked Bea.

"We know as much as you do." Ivan sounded sad. "In fact, we even went back to the mine to see if we could find a way back home. My friend, Calvin, who you guys destroyed, attempted to blow a hole in the mine. We thought we'd be able to create a portal, but it didn't work. We are stuck here, and we want to go back home and live under the sea."

"So do we," said Bea.

Brett realized Ivan and Calvin had caused the explosion in the mine. He reasoned with Ivan, "Since we all want to go back home, why don't we work together instead of spending all of our time battling each other?"

Ivan paused as he thought about this question. He wasn't sure how to respond. He never had to answer a question before; he was usually the one asking questions. He just stared at Brett and tried to think of a response. He knew Mikayla wouldn't want him working with a person who lived in the Overworld. She often told him that everyone who lived in the Overworld was an enemy.

"Aren't you going to answer me?" asked Brett.

Still Ivan remained silent.

Bea asked him, "What orders did Mikayla give you?"

"Same as you, I bet." He could answer this question. It was an easy one because it didn't involve making a decision. "She told me to capture everyone who lived in the Overworld."

"But didn't we look familiar?" asked Vera. "You must have seen us. We have orange hair. There are a bunch of us that Mikayla sent out in the wooden boat."

"She told us to capture you too. She wanted us to destroy you and everyone on the ship," explained Ivan.

"Why?" Bea was horrified.

"Because she felt that you guys weren't following orders. You spent too much time looking for buried treasure and following explorer maps."

As Ivan spoke, Calvin sprinted toward them. His green hair flopped in his face as he swung his sword at Vera.

"Stop!" Ivan called out. He was surprised this came from his mouth. He had never ordered anyone to do anything in his life.

"What?" Calvin was confused.

"Stop attacking her!" demanded Ivan.

Vera leaped at Calvin, piercing his arm with her diamond sword.

"You stop too!" screamed Ivan. "Everyone stop fighting! Please!"

The word *please* seemed to stick in the air, and everyone put their swords down.

Ivan said, "Calvin, I just found out that nobody wants to be here. We are all stuck in a time period that we don't want to be in, and we all have the same goal."

"I'm not," Grant said. "I am from here. I want to stay here and settle my towns."

"You can stay," said Ivan. "But will you help us get back?"

"Yes," said Grant.

Vera pulled a bottle of milk from her inventory and handed it Ivan. "Drink this and get your energy back, my sea-loving friend."

Calvin was still a bit confused, but he said, "If everyone here is trying to get back home, I will join you guys."

As they talked and tried to come up with a plan to get back home, the sky turned dark and thunder boomed throughout the Overworld. A zombie ripped Grant's door from its hinges, and the gang sprinted toward the smelly beast that reached for them with extended arms.

Brett held his breath as he battled the undead beast. When they destroyed the zombie, they sprinted outside to find a never-ending sea of zombies fill the land that would one day become Meadow Mews.

"We're outnumbered," said Ivan.

9
NIGHT BUILDING

They battled the zombies on a soggy ground. Bea slipped in a puddle and brushed the water off, then got up and struck a zombie. The stench coupled with the rain made the battle more uncomfortable; however, Brett smiled as he struck a zombie.

"Are you smiling?" Joe asked after he caught a glimpse of Brett.

Brett confessed, "It's because we are all working together. I was so worried we would be battling each other, but now we are all going to work together to make our way back home. Maybe once we are there, we can stop Mikayla."

"Stop Mikayla?" Ivan asked as he overheard Brett and Joe talk. He slammed his diamond sword into a vacant-eyed zombie.

"Yes," he said while leaping at two zombies and destroying both of them.

Bea sprinted in between them. "You guys can't talk! We have to stop this zombie invasion."

Brett agreed. He didn't want to continue the conversation about Mikayla, but Ivan had other ideas.

"He was just talking about stopping Mikayla," said Ivan as he pointed at Brett with one hand and struck a zombie with another.

"So?" Bea asked. "She is the reason we are stuck in this time period. She forced me to go on a boat and travel the world attacking villages. Then she wanted to capture or stop me because I enjoy looking for buried treasure. That isn't fair. She shouldn't have control over me. I realize now that I am not in her time period that I am free to make my own decisions, and I am enjoying it."

Ivan took in all of Bea's words. He hadn't thought about it that way, and he was beginning to see Bea's point. He struck another zombie. Two zombies leaped at Ivan, and he swung his sword at them. As he destroyed the zombies, he could hear a voice call out behind him.

"You have betrayed me," the voice said.

He turned around, but there was nobody there. He swung his sword at another zombie. He was growing tired. As flesh oozed from the zombie that stood inches from him, Ivan felt as if he was going to be sick.

Bea lunged at the zombie next to Ivan, destroying it. As he uttered, "Thank you," the sun began to shine, and the zombies disappeared.

The gang walked back to Grant's house. Joe and Brett helped Grant repair his door, and everyone piled into Grant's small living room. There were so many people in the living room that the weight from the guests made a hole in the living room floor, and Bea and Calvin fell into through the trapdoor on the floor.

"Are you okay?" Grant rushed toward them. He helped Bea and Grant out of the small room underneath his living room.

Calvin nodded his head.

"Yeah," Bea said as she took a sip from a potion to regain her strength. "What happened?"

"I use that space to hide stuff. Now you know my secrets," joked Grant. He apologized again for the incident and said, "As you guys can see, my place is way too small for everyone to stay here. Maybe we should build a home next to mine where everyone can stay."

Vera looked outside. It would be dark again soon. "We have to build something fast."

Brett thought about Poppy. She was probably wondering where he was and wondering why he wasn't on Helen's farm or getting ready to plan her rooftop farm. He wished she could be there to help them build the house, because she could build the best structures in no time. As they walked outside, they gathered all of their supplies from their inventories.

They all discussed plans for the house until a voice called out. "Brett!"

Brett couldn't believe it. It was Poppy. Her braids swayed as she hurtled through the meadow.

"How did you get here?"

"There's a new portal," she said breathlessly.

"Where?"

"The Nether," she said.

"What's the Nether?" asked Calvin.

"It's hard to explain," said Joe.

"What's going on in Meadow Mews?" asked Brett. He pointed to Vera and Bea. "Are their friends still attacking the town?"

"Yes," she said. "It's awful."

Joe and Calvin had started to build the side of the house when two block-carrying Endermen walked past them. Ivan tried not to lock eyes with the lanky Endermen, but it was too late. One of the Endermen unleashed a deafening high-pitched shriek, and Joe called out, "Sprint toward the water!"

Ivan did, and when he jumped into the water, he felt as if he was back at home. He missed the feeling of being immersed in water. He watched the Enderman jump in after him and be destroyed.

Ivan sipped a potion of Water Breathing and went deeper into the ocean. As he swam underneath the ocean, he saw fish swim past, and he felt at peace. In the distance he spotted a guardian, and he swam to the surface. Right before he reached the surface, he heard the same voice call out, "You have betrayed me."

When he reached the land, he sprinted in the darkness back to the area near Grant's house. The new house was almost complete. He heard Bea and Vera talking as they placed the windows on the house.

"I heard someone call out, 'You have betrayed me,' and when I turned around, they were gone," said Bea.

"I had that happen to me too," said Vera.

"That just happened when I was in the ocean," Ivan added, "and it happened once before too."

"Do you think it could be Mikayla?"

"I don't know," said Ivan. "The voice was faint, and I couldn't make out who was speaking."

Joe exclaimed, "We have a door! I think the house is complete."

They gathered inside and crafted beds. Joe looked at the bed and yawned. "It's been days. I can't believe I am finally going to sleep." He was he first person to climb into bed. He pulled the wool covers over himself and drifted off to sleep.

As Bea climbed into her bed, she heard a voice call out, "You betrayed me."

"Who said that?" she called out, but everyone was asleep.

10

NETHER REPEAT THIS

The sun was shining in their eyes, and everyone awoke. Brett was excited to wake up and see Poppy standing above him. He actually wondered if he had dreamed her return, but as she handed him an apple for breakfast, he knew it was real.

"Thanks." Brett smiled and took a bite of the apple. He chewed and then said, "Tell me again how you got here. What happened in the Nether?"

Everyone crowded around Poppy as she spoke. "Meadow Mews was under attack."

Bea interrupted, "It was being attacked by the other orange-haired people, right?"

"Yes," Poppy clarified, "and they were attacking me. I saw Nancy. She was building a portal to the Nether with a few other people. They were low on potions and they were tired of battle, so they were making their escape to the Nether."

Joe remarked, "You know its bad when you have to escape to the Nether."

"I know," said Poppy. "It's awful there."

"We have to get back to Meadow Mews," said Brett.

"Yes," said Poppy, "and I think we can get back there if we build a portal to the Nether."

"How?" asked Helen.

"When I was with Nancy, I found a fortress that had a portal. I think we can use that to get back to our time period," explained Poppy.

"We once came upon a portal in a Nether fortress that brought us to the past. How can we be sure that this portal will bring us to the future?" asked Brett.

"We have to try. It's our only hope," said Helen.

Ivan agreed, "We thought we could get back to our time period by blowing up a portion of the mine, but that didn't work. We should try this, because we have to try every option, even if it's a place I've never been."

Helen explained that there were many hostile mobs in the Nether and that they had to constantly look up for ghasts and blazes. She also told them to be mindful of the lava.

"I don't care how dangerous the Nether is," said Calvin, "I just want to find my way back home."

The gang followed Poppy outside as she pulled obsidian from her inventory and began to craft the portal. "I don't have enough supplies," she said, "Does anybody have obsidian?"

Brett and Joe were the only ones who had some, and they helped Poppy complete the portal. Everyone huddled together on the portal as the purple mist surrounded them. They emerged in the Nether, right next to a large lava waterfall.

Ivan, Calvin, Bea, and Vera stuck together. They stood inches from one another as they explored the Nether.

"This place is so hot," Ivan remarked as sweat formed on his forehead.

"This is nothing like our world under the sea," said Bea.

A group of ghasts flew toward them, and Poppy told everyone to take out their bow and arrows. "I can't believe I am instructing people on how to battle in the Nether. This is my least favorite place in the world, and I am not a fighter at all—I'm a builder."

"That gives me lots of hope," said Ivan as he awkwardly shot an arrow at the ghast and missed it. The ghast's fireball landed next to his feet and he jumped back to avoid getting singed.

"You can do it," said Poppy as she shot an arrow at the ghast, destroying it and grabbing the ghast tear.

Ivan didn't believe Poppy. He shot another arrow and missed again. A fireball fell at his feet, burning his toes. "Ouch!" he cried out in pain as he lost a heart.

"Try again," Poppy said.

Ivan took a deep breath and aimed at the ghast. He shot the arrow and it pierced the ghast, destroying it.

"Grab the ghast tear!" Poppy exclaimed.

Ivan picked up the ghast tear and placed it in his inventory.

"You earned that." She smiled as the gang annihilated the remaining ghasts.

As they walked through the Nether, Poppy asked Bea and Vera, "So you're on our side now?"

Bea and Vera looked at each other. Bea didn't feel like she was on any side. She knew that she didn't want to be controlled by Mikayla, but she also didn't feel as if she belonged to their community. She just wanted to be free. She said, "If you mean, am I going to break free of Mikayla, then yes. I just want to live my life without her ordering me around or punishing me for stopping to look for buried treasure."

"I get it," said Poppy. "Nobody wants to be bossed around."

Vera agreed. She was still in shock that Ivan and Calvin were sent to capture them and they were going to be punished for their mild treasure-hunting activities. It didn't make sense. They had provided Mikayla with riches from across the Overworld, and now she was upset because they wanted to do something on their own.

Calvin and Ivan both agreed they'd had enough of Mikayla. Ivan said, "When I get back to my time period. I will work to stop Mikayla so everyone who lives under the sea can live without fear."

As Ivan said these words, he heard a faint voice call out, "You have betrayed me."

He looked around the Nether, but nobody was there. "Did you hear that?" he asked the others.

"Hear what?" asked Poppy.

Before anyone could respond, Helen called out, "A Nether fortress."

The gang sprinted toward the fortress, but as they made their way there, they saw a group of people wearing masks.

"It's Mikayla's army," gasped Bea.

"They will destroy us for taking off our masks," said Bea.

"And for betraying Mikayla," added Vera.

"Don't worry," Ivan comforted them. "We have new friends now, and we will work together to stop them."

"I hope so," said Bea.

"You'll see," Calvin remarked as he charged toward the masked soldiers. "We will defeat them."

The gang clutched their diamond swords and swung at the masked army. With two hits, one of the soldiers was destroyed.

"We got this," said Ivan.

Everyone hoped this was true.

11

FIERY ESCAPES

The four soldiers that guarded the fortress were destroyed and the group could finally enter the fortress, but they were stopped when three blazes rose up from the ground and shot fireballs at the gang.

"Should I use my bow and arrow?" Ivan asked Poppy.

"Or a snowball," said Poppy.

"What's that?" asked Calvin.

"I'll explain later," said Poppy as she threw a snowball at a blaze, destroying it. Poppy, Brett, Joe, Grant, and Helen battled the blazes as Ivan and the others tried to help, but they weren't yet skilled enough to battle well in the Nether.

The blazes were gone, and they sprinted into the fortress. Poppy heard people talking. "Quiet," she whispered to her friends. "I hear voices."

The gang tried to remain as quiet as possible as

they made their way through the fortress. They walked down a narrow hall, and Poppy heard a voice call out, "Poppy! Help!"

"Nancy?" Poppy sped down the hall, looking in each room for Nancy. As she looked in the final room, she felt something on her shoulder. She turned around and was standing face-to-face with a wither skeleton.

The fortress was full of wither skeletons, and she struck the beast with her diamond sword and destroyed the Nether mob. It dropped its stone sword, and she picked it up as she attempted to battle another wither skeleton.

"Poppy!" the voice called out again. "Help!"

"Nancy?" asked Poppy as she struck the wither skeleton with her sword, but it didn't impact the beast.

"Yes," Nancy called out. "I need your help!"

Poppy couldn't reply. She had one heart left and two wither skeletons surrounding her. Helen dashed toward Poppy, thrusting her diamond sword at the wither skeletons and destroying them. She handed Poppy a glass of milk.

Poppy took a sip and said, "Nancy is here."

"She is?" asked Helen. "Where?"

"We have to find her," Poppy replied as she raced through the fortress, calling out her friend's name.

In the other section of the Nether fortress, magma cubes surrounded Joe, Grant, and Brett, and they had to battle the slimy boxy cubes while also explaining how to battle them to their friends, who only knew about life under the sea.

Bea slammed her diamond sword into one of the cubes. "What?" she exclaimed. "You strike them and then it creates more of these blocks?"

"They break into pieces," explained Brett.

"But the pieces can attack you. This is crazy." She struck the smaller cubes with her sword and was relieved when she destroyed a tiny cube. Her relief was short-lived, because she looked up and spotted at least seven more magma cubes in the room.

The gang plunged their swords into the cubes. Then Poppy rushed in and screamed, "Nancy!"

"Is Nancy here?" Joe asked.

"I bet that means the portal is here," said Brett. "We have to destroy these magma cubes so we can get to Nancy."

They were battling a never-ending group of magma cubes, and they were down to a handful of cubes when Nancy bolted into the room.

"Help! They are going to destroy me!" Nancy cried.

"Who?" asked Brett as he obliterated a magma cube.

Nancy didn't have to respond. Within seconds the room was flooded with masked criminals. One of the criminals spotted Bea.

"Traitor! You're the treasure-hunting traitor!" the masked criminal hollered.

"She took off her mask! You've betrayed Mikayla!" another criminal called out in disbelief.

The criminals spotted Vera in the distance. "Another one!"

"I can't believe they took off their masks," said the criminal.

Bea slammed her sword into a magma cube as she rushed toward Mikayla's soldiers. "Mikayla is controlling you."

"She is our leader!" declared one of the criminals.

"No, she is your controller, and she doesn't care about you. She just wants you to work for her. She tried to imprison me because I like to look for buried treasure even though I was planning on giving her the treasure I had found." Tears formed in Bea's eyes as she spoke.

"You are our prisoner," asserted the criminal. "We are bringing you back to Mikayla."

"No, you are *our* prisoners," said Calvin as he and Ivan sprinted in and hit two magmas with their swords. "Now lead us to the portal."

The criminals spoke, but nobody could hear them. The room filled with more magma cubes, and five wither skeletons spawned in the room. As the group battled these mobs, a crop of blazes flew into the room and began to shoot fireballs at them. They were battling three different mobs in a small room in a Nether fortress. Bea had one heart left when she sprinted past a barrage of fireballs and toward one of the soldiers.

Vera, Bea, Ivan, and Calvin were getting a fast lesson on how to battle all of the mobs of the Nether, and it wasn't easy. They were losing hearts, and the battle was intense.

Bea didn't want to waste her energy battling the

mobs when she really wanted to stop Mikayla's soldiers. She struck one of the criminals with her diamond sword. "Show us where the portal is," she demanded.

Nancy tore toward them. "I think I can find it," she said as she destroyed a wither skeleton and quickly picked up the stone sword.

"Let's make our way to the portal," Brett instructed his friends.

"Follow me," Nancy called out breathlessly as they fled past the mobs.

They rushed toward a room down the hall. The minute they entered the room, Brett knew they had found the portal. There was an icy breeze that felt as if they were standing by the ocean in the middle of the winter. The cold burned his cheeks, and he knew that the portal was just inches away. He watched as Nancy hopped into the portal. Brett braced himself for the cold. He knew there was no way to prepare for it. Whenever he fell down a portal, he froze and his skin got goose bumps. He wanted the frigid air to turn warm. He wanted to land in his old time period. As he fell deeper into the portal, he thought about Grant and how he was time traveling for the first time. If they landed in their time period, Grant would see how Meadow Mews had developed. He'd also find out that nobody had heard from him in ages. Brett wondered how Grant would take that news.

12

BATTLE UNDER THE SEA

The portal put them on a beach. Brett landed in the sand with a thump, right after Nancy. The others fell from the portal, and soon they were all crowded together on the beach. The sun beat down on them, and Brett was happy to feel the warmth on his skin.

"Is everyone here?" asked Brett.

Grant was confused. He looked around, trying to place where they were, but he couldn't. "What time period are we in? Where are we?" His voice cracked. He appeared nervous.

"We have no idea," said Helen as she looked around. "Nothing looks familiar to me."

"I don't recognize anything," said Bea, "and I have been on many beaches because I love looking for buried treasure in the sand."

"I have an idea," Vera said as she pulled out a potion

of Water Breathing. "Let's go under the sea and see if we can find anybody we know."

"But everyone under the sea wants to capture you. You are a traitor, and Mikayla will make you her prisoner," said Ivan.

Calvin reminded her, "We were sent here to capture you and Vera."

Vera said, "And look at how the criminals reacted when they saw you in the Nether fortress."

Bea sipped the potion. "This is the reason I have to go under the sea. I have to defend myself, and I have to confront Mikayla. I can't let her bully me and everyone else who lives under the sea."

Grant eyed the potion. He had just traveled through a portal for the first time in his life, and now he had to go under the sea. He wasn't familiar with underwater life, and he was scared. He looked over at Bea, who fearlessly drank the potion. She was ready to battle the person who wanted to imprison her. Grant wanted to be like Bea. He wanted to be brave, but he was scared. He took a sip of the potion and looked over at Joe. "You will stick by me when we are under the sea, right?"

"Yes," Joe said as he gulped the potion. He was also scared about going under the sea and was glad to have Grant by his side.

Grant was about to pause and run away when he heard a loud thump. He turned around to see Mikayla's soldiers fall from the portal. He looked at the sea all of his friends had jumped in. The only person he could see was Joe. Joe was floating in the water and he called to Grant, "Come on."

Grant felt like his heart was going to beat out of his chest as he jumped into the water. He was surprised at how peaceful he felt as he swam deeper into the ocean. A school of yellow pufferfish swam past, and he wanted to reach out and touch them, but he didn't. He knew he shouldn't disturb them. He spotted tropical fish swimming below. The brightly colored fish appeared almost magical and were a stunning sight.

"This is gorgeous," Grant told Joe.

"I know. I didn't think it would be this lush and colorful. I love seeing all of the fish swim past us," said Joe.

Grant was glad he drank the potion and was able to experience life under the sea. However, he still wanted to know what time period they were in and if they were in the future. He was fearful he'd never be able to make it back to the past. He calmed down as he swam past a group of tropical fish, but his heart raced as he spotted something in the distance.

"What's that?" Grant asked. A green man in the distance looked as if he were covered in seaweed. "Or shall I say *who* is that?"

Bea called out, "It's a Drowned. They are like zombies of the ocean. If you destroy them, you can sometimes get a trident, which is like the coolest weapon in the world. You can't even craft them. You can only get them when you destroy a Drowned."

Vera said, "We have to swim toward the Drowned

and destroy it. We need as many weapons as we can use to battle Mikayla."

The ocean folk swam toward the Drowned. Each of them wanted to battle the underwater zombie.

Four more drowned mobs spawned on the ocean floor. Ivan said, "Great, we're so lucky we have more to battle."

"I wouldn't call that luck," Grant said.

Calvin swam toward the Drowned, pulled out his sword, and swung at the undead mob. Grant watched as the Drowned was destroyed and dropped rotten flesh that was similar to a zombie's.

"So annoying," said Calvin. "I wanted a trident."

Grant swam toward a Drowned and pulled out his diamond sword. He was glad the Drowned didn't have the same odor as a zombie. He struck the Drowned with his diamond sword, but he wasn't able to destroy it. He hit the Drowned two more times and destroyed it. He picked up a trident on the ocean floor.

"You got a trident! Good job!" exclaimed Bea.

As they battled the remaining Drowned, a voice called out, "You have betrayed me."

Bea turned around and saw Mikayla swimming toward her.

13

THIS IS HARDCORE

Mikayla had flaming red hair and wore a crown. She wasn't known to ever leave her ocean monument, so Bea was shocked that she was swimming toward them. Bea swam toward her. She was afraid of Mikayla, but she was going to face the queen and let her know that Bea had the right to look for buried treasure. Bea also wanted Mikayla to know that she was terrorizing everyone under the sea.

"You have returned," Mikayla called out, "and now you will be punished."

"She hasn't done anything wrong," hollered Ivan.

"Ivan," Mikayla said, "you surprise me. I sent you to capture the traitors, not side with them."

"Well, I did." Ivan swam toward Mikayla with his diamond sword. Calvin followed behind him.

Calvin said, "You are outnumbered."

"Calvin," Mikayla laughed, "you too? I thought you were smarter than that."

"You're going to be destroyed," said Calvin. "We have you cornered."

Mikayla laughed even louder, and the water shook. "Seriously? You think I'd let myself be trapped?" She called out, "Soldiers, attack."

The second these words fell from her lips, the gang was surrounded by hundreds of masked criminals. The soldiers swam around them and shot arrows.

"Now I have many prisoners." Mikayla laughed again as she instructed the soldiers to stop shooting. "I've placed them on hardcore mode, and I don't want them to be destroyed forever. I'd rather watch them spend the rest of their days in my prison, where I can visit them and laugh."

"Should we put them in the prison?" asked one of the soldiers.

"You have to ask?" Mikayla was annoyed.

The gang reluctantly swam toward the ocean monument. Once they were inside, they were led through a series of rooms until they reached a room with bars.

"This is where you will stay," said Mikayla as she slammed the bars shut.

She ordered the soldiers to provide the prisoners with a lifetime supply of potions of Water Breathing. "I need to know that they will be here. I don't want any one of them being destroyed."

She watched as they drank the potion of Water Breathing. Bea asked, "Why don't you just take us off of hardcore mode? I have no idea why you want to keep us down here forever. It doesn't make sense."

"You have no right to state your opinion. This is all your fault," declared Mikayla.

"My fault?" Bea asked. "Just because I wanted to look for treasure? Now, that doesn't make sense. I was going to give you the treasure I found too."

"You think that giving me the treasure would make everything okay? You can't give me anything because I already own everything you have. I am in charge in the ocean world. Everything here is mine. That reminds me." She looked at Grant. "Give me your trident right now."

"Don't do it, Grant," cried Bea.

"Bea," Mikayla screamed. "You don't tell anybody what to do when you are in my world. You were always such a troublemaker."

Grant pulled the trident from his inventory. He didn't want to give it to the queen, but he also didn't want to be destroyed. They were on hardcore mode, and that was serious. He clutched the trident as she opened the gate and swam toward him. Mikayla had several soldiers swimming behind her, ready to stop any of the gang from escaping this underwater prison.

"Give me the trident," she demanded.

"No!" Grant surprised himself.

"Since you are new, you have no idea how powerful I am, so I will give you a moment to collect your thoughts and understand what you are saying. Then you will give me the trident."

Grant struck the queen with the trident. She lost a heart and screamed in pain, then screamed, "Soldiers, destroy him forever!"

Bea cried out, "Stop! Leave Grant alone." Bea tried to reason with Grant. "Just give her the trident."

Grant wouldn't listen. Instead he struck Mikayla again, which infuriated her, and she swung her diamond sword at him, and he vanished.

"Grant!" Brett called out.

Helen screamed, "Do you know what you just did?"

Mikayla replied, "Of course, I was the one who did it. I destroyed your annoying friend. It doesn't really matter."

"It doesn't matter?" Helen screamed. "By destroying Grant, you have changed the history of the Overworld forever. He was a person who settled most of the towns that you were looting."

"That means nothing to me. He was a person who disobeyed me, and that is all that matters," said Mikayla.

"All that matters?" Helen was upset. "What is wrong with you?"

"I should ask you the same question," said Mikayla, and then she ordered the soldiers to destroy Helen.

"What did you do to Helen?" asked Nancy.

"It seems like you guys don't learn anything. Do you all want to be destroyed? If you do, I will destroy all of you." She looked at Bea. "Except for you. I want to keep you here so everyone in the ocean world can see what happens when you decide to do your own thing."

"You are terrible," said Bea.

"Say what you want," Mikayla laughed. "It will get you nowhere. I don't care to destroy you. You will be here forever."

"I will get the people to turn against you," Bea threatened.

"Do you think that scares me?" Mikayla asked.

"I hope it does," Bea replied.

"You are too funny," Mikayla giggled.

"I just want to—" But Bea stopped talking.

"Finally, you are doing something right." Mikayla smiled.

Bea was upset. She had lost two friends, and she was stuck in the ocean prison for the rest of her days. She had a lot of things to say to Mikayla, but she decided to say nothing. She wanted Mikayla to swim away so they could plot their escape.

14

WHERE ARE YOU?

"We have to get out of here," said Bea.

"I can't believe Mikayla destroyed Grant and Helen," Nancy cried.

"I know," Bea said. "I'm sorry, it's my fault."

"It's not your fault," Brett told her. "You didn't have anything to do with this. This is all Mikayla, and you're right: we have to escape, and we have to stop her."

Poppy said, "I wonder if Meadow Mews even exists anymore. I mean, if Grant isn't alive to found it, then we might be returning to a land that doesn't exist."

Joe said, "We don't even know if we will ever get out of here. We shouldn't focus on Meadow Mews. We have to focus on how to escape."

Vera looked through her inventory. "You know what's weird? Mikayla didn't even empty our inventories, which means we have lots of resources."

"You're right," said Joe as he looked through his inventory.

Ivan pulled out a pickaxe. "Let's dig our way out," he said, but as he spoke, four of Mikayla's soldiers swam to the prison bars. He stopped talking.

"We are the prison guards, and we will also provide you with food," said the guard.

"We hope you like fish," the other guard said as she handed them some rotten fish.

The fish smelled awful, and although Poppy had no food in her inventory, she didn't take it. "Won't we get sick if we eat this?" she asked the guards.

"Only one way to find out," replied one of the guards.

Poppy couldn't eat the fish. The smell was so rancid that she couldn't even be in the same room as the fish. The others agreed, and they threw the fish outside of the prison bars. This annoyed the soldiers. One of the soldiers picked up the rotten fish and swam away to dispose of it.

Brett had a plan, but he wasn't sure how he could bring it up to his friends. There were soldiers watching their every move. He swam next to Joe and whispered in his ear. "We need to attack the soldiers. We have to use our arrows."

Joe whispered this plan into Ivan's ear. As everyone whispered Brett's idea into their neighbor's ear, Brett worried this would turn into a game of telephone. Usually at the end of a game of telephone, the message got jumbled and somebody misheard it. This meant the final person usually never heard the original message. This wasn't a game, and if the final person didn't the message, something bad could happen.

He watched as the message was passed from one person to another. His heart beat fast. When the last person got the message, Brett picked out his arrow from his inventory. However, he didn't even have to use it, because a group of Drowned mobs spawned outside the prison bars, and they attacked the soldiers.

The soldiers weren't prepared for the attack. They were taken by surprise, and one of the Drowned destroyed two soldiers. There weren't many soldiers left, and Brett and the gang used this opportunity to shoot arrows at the soldiers and the Drowned.

The arrows destroyed the soldiers and the Drowned. Brett could see a trident on the ocean ground. He put his hand through the bars, but he couldn't reach it.

Bea said, "We can't worry about things like tridents. We have to use our pickaxes and dig our way out of here. We must escape right now."

Everyone agreed, and they dug as fast as they could. Soon they had a large hole in the ground. They swam inside the hole, and Brett immediately felt a breeze of freezing cold air.

"There's another portal," he exclaimed, but his words weren't heard. He was in the portal traveling to an unknown time period. The combination of being wet and in the cold air transformed his arms into ice cubes. Brett was convinced he was going to freeze to death. He couldn't worry about where he was going to land. He was too concerned with staying alive. He also knew that they might still be on hardcore mode, which made this journey even scarier.

He fell to the ground, but he didn't get a break from the cold. They were in the cold taiga, and he was the first to fall into the snow. He wished he had a jacket. Poppy was the second person to fall out of the portal, and she stood up and looked around. "Where are we?" she asked.

"I have no idea," said Brett. "It could be the past or it could be the future."

The rest of the gang fell into the snow. Ivan, Calvin, Bea, and Vera looked at the ground, "What is this?" Calvin asked as he picked up the snow and put it in his hand, shaping it into a ball.

"This is snow," said Poppy.

Brett added, "And you've just created a snowball."

"This biome is amazing," said Vera. "It's the best."

"Well, I'm glad you're having fun," said Poppy, "because we have to figure out where we are."

Nancy pulled out a map. "Maybe this could help. It's an old treasure map that I have. It looks like this cold taiga biome is on it."

The group crowded around Nancy to stare at the map when they heard a familiar voice call out.

"Nancy! Over here!"

"Who said that?" asked Nancy.

"Nancy! Brett! Help!" another voice called out.

"What's going on?" asked Brett. He recognized the familiar voices, but he couldn't believe it.

"Where are you?" asked Nancy.

The group sprinted toward the sound of the voices and found Helen and Grant standing next to a large mountain of snow.

15

REVENGE

"We weren't on hardcore mode," explained Grant. "I awoke in my house and Helen awoke next door."

"How are you guys here?" asked Poppy.

"We were searching for a portal," said Helen, "and since every portal seems to be cold, we thought we'd find one in the cold taiga biome."

"How far are we from Meadow Mews?" asked Joe.

"Not far," replied Grant.

"I have a feeling that we should go back to the mine. I think we have to figure out why the mine stopped producing any gems. I just believe if we figure out who is going to destroy the mine or how the mine will be destroyed, we will find our answers."

Brett agreed that they might find answers in the stronghold, which was located in the mine. They followed Grant and Helen toward the Meadow Mews, and once they reached the mine, they were shocked to see it filled with Mikayla's masked soldiers.

The gang took out their diamond swords and struck the soldiers, but it seemed as if there was a never-ending supply of soldiers.

"How are we going to destroy these soldiers?" asked Helen. "There are too many there."

"They aren't as powerful as you think," said Bea. "If they were, you'd be gone. They couldn't even put you on hardcore mode, and Mikayla is so petty that she was going to imprison me for trying to search for buried treasure. If she was capable of creating a strong army, she wouldn't have been worried about me. She has controlled the people in the ocean world for so long, they have no idea how to think for themselves. Soldiers who can't think for themselves are easy to battle. If we destroy one, we can destroy them all," Bea said as she raced toward the soldiers and began to destroy them with her diamond sword.

"There is no escape!" she called out at the top of her lungs.

Bea struck two soldiers, destroying them. Her friends joined her in battle, but the sun was beginning to set, and a group of skeletons and zombies spawned. The skeletons shot arrows at the gang, and the horrid-smelling zombies lumbered toward the gang and the soldiers. They were in the midst of one large battle between the soldiers and the mobs.

Ivan rushed toward Brett's side and said, "I have TNT in the stronghold. I had it because we were using it to make a hole in the ground to create a portal. Should we use it to blow up the mine and destroy the soldiers?"

Brett slammed his sword into a skeleton and picked up the dropped bone that fell to the ground when it was destroyed.

"I think that sounds like the only idea that could work, but how can we get into the stronghold? It's filled with soldiers," said Brett as he plunged his sword into the belly of a vacant-eyed zombie.

"I'm not sure," said Ivan as he shot an arrow at a soldier. "Keep fighting and tell the others."

"Sounds like a plan," said Brett.

Brett raced toward Poppy to tell her about the plan. They had to battle and make their way into the stronghold to get the TNT. Within minutes the entire gang knew the plan. Brett felt like this could work, and he was very optimistic.

There were about twenty soldiers in the mine. The soldiers used arrows, tridents, and diamond swords to attack the gang and whatever hostile mobs were in the mine. The gang fought the soldiers as they tried to make their way into the stronghold.

"We can do this," Brett said to Poppy. He thought about what Bea had said about the soldiers and how they all thought the same way. He slammed his sword into a soldier, and it was destroyed. He watched another soldier perish the same way. Bea was right. They didn't think for themselves, so all they could do was follow directions. Mikayla must have told them to destroy anyone who entered the mine and stronghold and not to leave. The soldiers stayed in the same place and fought from their positions. The gang struck them with diamond swords and splashed potions on them until they were all destroyed.

"We destroyed all of the soldiers in the mine!" declared Bea.

"Now we will destroy the rest in the stronghold," said Brett.

They sprinted deep into the stronghold until they found the TNT hidden in a dark corner. A pair of red eyes peered at them, and Ivan swung his sword at the cave spider that crawled next to the pile of TNT.

The gang grabbed the TNT, placed a large stack by the entrance to the stronghold, lit it, and ran.

Kaboom!

The stronghold was destroyed. They also placed a bunch of TNT in the mine.

Kaboom!

They stood outside the charred mine in the darkness. There were no more soldiers left, but a few hostile mobs lurked in the darkness. A spider jockey headed toward them.

Brett aimed his bow and arrow at the skeleton. "Bull's-eye," he said, and the skeleton was destroyed. Poppy charged the spider and struck it with her sword, destroying it.

The gang hurried back to the two houses and crawled into bed. They were exhausted. When they awoke, they were surprised to see Mikayla in the living room. She wasn't wearing her crown, and she was alone.

16

WATERY REUNION

"**Y**ou've destroyed my army," Mikayla announced. Yet she didn't sound upset; she sounded defeated.

"We destroyed the army forever?" Bea felt guilty. She didn't want to destroy anybody. She didn't think they were on hardcore mode. She had believed they would all return to the world under the sea and she would be able to stay on land with her new friends.

"Were they on hardcore mode?" questioned Brett.

"No," Mikayla replied.

This didn't make sense to Bea, and she wondered if Mikayla was trying to trick them. She didn't trust her. "Then how did we destroy them?"

"Look outside," she said.

Bea walked outside the house and was shocked to see all of the soldiers without their masks on. One of the soldiers said, "We aren't going to follow Mikayla anymore. We want to be free like you."

"What happened?" Bea wasn't sure what happened.

The unmasked soldier who had just spoken said, "We heard you saying that we were easy to battle because we don't think."

Another soldier said, "It was at that moment we decided that we needed to think for ourselves."

"Does this mean you are all going your separate ways?" asked Bea.

"Yes," replied one soldier.

Another said, "Today we are going to pick out our own skins. Then we will decide if we want to live under the sea or on land."

Bea was shocked that her words had that much power, and she was proud of the soldiers' actions. She said, "I am happy that you have chosen your own paths."

As she spoke, Mikayla walked out of the house. She handed her crown to Bea. "I am no longer the queen of the underwater world."

Bea held the crown. It was gold and much heavier than she imagined. She wanted to place it on her head. She was curious to see how it felt to be queen, but she knew that she'd never want that power over anybody else. Instead of trying on the crown, she handed the crown back to Mikayla. "Keep this in your inventory."

"What?" Mikayla was confused.

"You don't have to give it up. You just shouldn't wear it," she said.

Mikayla held the crown and then placed it in her inventory. Then she delivered a speech to her former army. "I want to apologize for my actions. I shouldn't have kept you from living the lives you wanted. I wish you luck on your new adventures."

One of the soldiers said, "We want to start our life in our time period. How do we get out of here?"

Mikayla confessed, "I don't know."

"Do you think we should go under the sea and see if we could find a portal?" questioned one of the soldiers.

"Let's see," said another, and the soldiers rushed the coast and jumped into the water. They swam deep into the ocean, but they didn't find a portal. They didn't even find an ocean monument. It seemed as if the sea was barren. Ivan said, "Perhaps this isn't the best idea. It doesn't seem like the sea is developed yet. Except for a few fish, there is really nothing down here."

The group swam to the surface and stood on the beach. They all had various ideas of where they might find a portal, but nobody was certain. As they spoke, raindrops fell from the sky and thunder boomed.

"Oh no," cried Helen. "A sun shower."

Within seconds skeletons and zombies spawned, and everyone was involved with the battle. Brett took a deep breath as he plunged his sword into a skeleton. As he picked up a dropped bone from the soggy ground, he looked up and saw everyone battling the mobs together, and he smiled. He was glad that there would be peace in the Overworld.

A smelly zombie lunged at Grant, and he lost a heart. He only had one heart left as he swung his sword at the undead beast. He was relieved when he destroyed the zombie and grabbed a bottle of milk to replenish his energy. As he took a sip, the sun came out, and everyone continued the conversation on how they might get back to their time period.

Grant suggested, "Maybe the way out is through the mine. Perhaps that's why the mine isn't working anymore. Maybe it was destroyed when it became a portal for hundreds of people?"

Everyone thought that was a good theory, and they jogged to the mine. But nobody felt the familiar cold breeze that emanated from the portal. They clutched their torches and searched every inch of the portal and the stronghold. The TNT had created gaping holes in the mine and the stronghold, and the gang peered into the holes, but they didn't see a portal.

"What are we going to do?" asked Helen.

Nobody answered.

17

POTENTIAL PORTALS

They walked out of the mine feeling defeated. Poppy said, "I wonder if we could find one in the cold taiga biome?"

Grant said, "That sounds like a good idea, but can we check the mine one more time? I feel a breeze."

"You feel a breeze?" asked Brett, and when he saw Grant nod his head, he dashed into the mine and searched for the portal. He felt cold air coming from a small hole in the ground and banged his pickaxe against the ground. The blocks gave way, and Brett fell down the portal. As he made his way deeper into the portal, his arms began to freeze and his teeth chattered, but he smiled the entire way. He was happy to be going home. The only thing that bothered him was that he didn't get to say goodbye to Grant. However, he knew that he would probably see the man again on another time-traveling adventure.

Brett didn't know that the portal closed right after he fell through. When he landed with a thump in the middle of Meadow Mews, the sun was shining, and it was peaceful. He waited for a while for Poppy, Joe, Helen, and the others, but nobody showed up.

Poppy was still in the past. She stood by the portal that had closed and questioned, "How are we going to get back home?"

Joe felt a mild breeze behind him, "Does anybody feel that breeze?"

Ivan said, "Yes, I do."

Together they rushed to the corner of the mine and began to knock against the wall where they had felt the cold air. They both fell into the portal and landed in Meadow Mews.

"Brett?" Joe hollered when he didn't see his friend. Then he hurried to Brett's house.

"You guys made it back to Meadow Mews," exclaimed Brett, and then he asked. "Where's Poppy?"

"It's weird," explained Ivan. "It seems like there are small portals and only a few people can travel through them."

Back in the mine, people kept feeling cool breezes, and eventually the entire mine had transformed from a place where one would find endless treasures to a depleted mine that had been used to transport every-one back to their original time period. The only person who stayed behind was Grant.

Grant inspected the portal. It was filled with holes. He walked around wondering if he would feel a cool breeze, but he never did. He knew he was meant to stay in the past to develop Meadow Mews, Farmer's Bay, and many other communities. Although he knew this was his place in the world, he was also sad to see his friends leave. He hoped he would see them again in the future.

Grant took one more look at the mine and smiled. Now he knew the story behind the mine, but he wasn't sure how he'd explain it to anybody in his time period. Nobody would believe him when he told folks that he had met time travelers and that there were people who lived underneath the sea. He laughed to himself when he thought about it and said, "Nope, there is no way anyone is going to believe me, so I will just say nothing."

Grant knew this would mean that people would make up their own stories about how and why the mine was emptied, and he was okay with that. It was rare to come across a mine that didn't have one precious stone in it. As he exited the mine for the last time, he smiled.

Grant had lots of work ahead of him. He had only heard snippets about what Meadow Mews was like in the future, but he did gather that it was a flourishing community. He knew he had to get to work. The first thing he wanted to construct was a library. He wanted to see the bookshelves lined with stories about history. However, he wasn't going to let the story of the mine get into a history book, because that was his secret.

As Grant walked toward his house, he spotted a woman with red hair walking toward him.

"Helen," he called out.

She stopped, "How do you know my name?"

He didn't want to tell her that he met her future self but said, "Good guess."

"I'd say that was a really good guess," she said.

"Do you need help with anything?" he asked.

"I'm looking for a place to build a shelter." She looked up at the sky. "It's getting dark, and I don't want to be attacked by hostile mobs."

Grant said, "I have a house not far from here. You can build one next to mine if you'd like. I am trying to start a town called Meadow Mews. You can be one of our first residents."

"That sounds great," Helen said.

As they walked toward Grant's house, Grant was happy to be reunited with Helen. He giggled when she asked, "I saw you standing by a mine. Is that mine good? I mean, can I go there tomorrow and mine for diamonds?"

"That mine isn't working. There is nothing in there," he replied.

"That's strange," remarked Helen.

"Yes," said Grant, "I'm not sure why it's depleted."

"Well," said Helen, "we'll have to find another mine."

"We will," said Grant as they reached his house. He looked out on the meadow. He couldn't wait to start constructing the town.

Helen looked at the plot of land where Grant suggested she build her home. "It looks like a great place to build a real home, and I'm going to leave a bunch of space for a farm."

18

THE GRASS IS ALWAYS GREENER

Brett was working on the farm when Helen told him about the day she built her house alongside Grant's.

"It's funny," she said. "I told him that I would make a farm here, and it took me this long to finally do it."

"I miss Grant," remarked Brett.

"Me too," added Joe.

Helen looked at the farm. She eyed the apple trees, which hadn't begun to grow apples. Everything was just planted, and she had to wait for them to grow.

Nancy walked over and commented on the farm, "Wow, you guys did a good job. I can't wait until everything is ripe. This is where I'm going to pick apples."

"You can help yourself to everything," remarked Helen.

Poppy ran over to the farm. "You guys are done, right?"

Joe and Brett looked at the farm. Brett confessed, "I'm never really done with the farm. There's always something to add."

"Is that a yes or a no?" asked Poppy.

"I guess it's a yes," Brett laughed. "We're done."

"Great," she said. "I need your help with the rooftop farm."

Helen said, "I am excited to see your next project. I can see how much work you've done on the skyscraper, Poppy."

The skyscraper looked as if it touched the clouds. It loomed high above Meadow Mews. There was still work to be done. Once it was completed there would be a large grand opening party. Many people from around the Overworld were going to celebrate the opening. The town even asked Poppy to build a hotel to house everyone who was scheduled to come.

"I'm not done with the skyscraper until you guys complete the rooftop farm," said Poppy.

Vera and Bea rushed toward Poppy. "Did you ask Brett yet?"

"No." Poppy smiled.

"Ask me what?" Brett questioned.

Vera blurted out, "We wanted to help you construct the farm. We want to learn how to be farmers."

Bea added, "Now that we are staying in the Overworld, we have to acquire new skills."

Brett said, "Of course you can help us."

Joe smiled. "The more the merrier."

Nancy remarked, "I thought you guys were treasure hunters."

"That's another skill I need to perfect. I hope we can go on a treasure hunt soon," said Bea.

"You can't go anywhere until this rooftop farm is complete," said Poppy.

Brett took out the plans for the new rooftop farm and showed them to Bea, Vera, Joe, and Poppy. They looked over the plans. Poppy said, "This is going to be better than I imagined."

Brett asked Helen and Nancy if they'd like to see the plans, but they shook their heads. Helen explained, "We want to be surprised."

Nancy said, "I really can't wait for the grand opening."

Poppy laughed. "Me too."

"I hope we don't fall down a portal before the opening," joked Brett.

"I wouldn't joke about that," said Joe.

The gang walked toward the skyscraper, and Poppy explained to Bea and Vera how an elevator worked.

"There's so much to learn about life on land," said Bea.

"Don't worry," said Poppy. "We're here to help you."

Bea smiled and said, "Thank you."

The sun was beginning to set, and the gang hurried toward the skyscraper.

"I crafted beds in the skyscraper," Poppy told them. "We can all stay there tonight."

Tomorrow they would start on the farm. They went to bed excited for the next day.

The End